THE
LANGUAGE
OF CATS

and Other Stories

THE
LANGUAGE
OF CATS
and Other Stories

* *
*

SPENCER HOLST

The McCall Publishing Company

NEW YORK

To my father, to my son
LAWRENCE SPENCER HOLST
SEBASTIAN SPENCER HOLST
A father's pride is his son's rejoicing

Published simultaneously in Canada by
Doubleday Canada Ltd., Toronto

Library of Congress Catalog Card Number: 79–134479

SBN 8415-0079-7

Design by Tere LoPrete

The McCall Publishing Company
230 Park Avenue
New York, New York 10017

Printed in the United States of America

Contents

✳ ✳
✳

"... that, in general, from the violation of a few simple laws of humanity arises the wretchedness of mankind—that as a species we have in our possession the as yet unwrought elements of content—and that, even now in the present darkness and madness of all thought on the great question of the social condition, it is not impossible that man, the individual, under certain unusual and highly fortuitous conditions, may be happy."

EDGAR ALLAN POE
—*The Domain of Arnheim*

THE
LANGUAGE
OF CATS

and Other Stories

The Zebra Storyteller

ONCE upon a time there was a Siamese cat who pretended to be a lion and spoke inappropriate Zebraic.

That language is whinnied by the race of striped horses in Africa.

Here now: An innocent zebra is walking in a jungle and approaching from another direction is the little cat; they meet.

"Hello there!" says the Siamese cat in perfectly pronounced Zebraic, "It certainly is a pleasant day, isn't it? The sun is shining, the birds are singing, isn't the world a lovely place to live today!"

The zebra is so astonished at hearing a Siamese cat speaking like a zebra, why—he's just fit to be tied.

So the little cat quickly ties him up, kills him, and drags the better parts of the carcass back to his den.

The cat successfully hunted zebras many months in this manner, dining on filet mignon of zebra every night, and from the better hides he made bow neckties and wide belts after the fashion of the decadent princes of the Old Siamese court.

He began boasting to his friends he was a lion, and he gave them as proof the fact that he hunted zebras.

The delicate noses of the zebras told them there was really no lion in the neighborhood. The zebra deaths caused many to avoid the region. Superstitious, they decided the woods were haunted by the ghost of a lion.

One day the storyteller of the zebras was ambling, and through his mind ran plots for stories to amuse the other zebras, when suddenly his eyes brightened, and he said, "That's it! I'll tell a story about a Siamese cat who learns to speak our language! What an idea! That'll make 'em laugh!"

Just then the Siamese cat appeared before him, and said, "Hello there! Pleasant day today, isn't it!"

The zebra storyteller wasn't fit to be tied at hearing a cat speaking his language, because he'd been thinking about that very thing.

He took a good look at the cat, and he didn't know why, but there was something about his looks he didn't like, so he kicked him with a hoof and killed him.

That is the function of the storyteller.

Mona Lisa Meets Buddha

✳   ✳
✳

Up in heaven the curtains fluttered, the curtains fluttered, the curtains fluttered, and the Mona Lisa entered at one end of a small hall, which was hung with many curtains.

Up in heaven the curtains fluttered, fluttered, fluttered, and the Buddha entered the hall at the other end.

They smiled.

Another Impostor

* *
*

ONCE upon a time a millionaire playboy burned his face off in an automobile accident.

After that he became a recluse, he stopped seeing all his friends, and he lived up in his big stone house on large grounds which he never left.

Wild rumors ran about him, about the splendor of his life, about rare wines he drank, and women, women were there, it was whispered, and they said he had great collections of things like art and books and drums and daggers and they said he kept live smooth fish in his secret swimming pool someplace deep within the walls of his impenetrable house.

His theater was on the roof and he'd hire whole Broadway casts to play for him there, and stars of the ballet and concert stage to come and perform for him.

He never spoke to any of the stars who came into his house, but they would see him occasionally over the footlights with a black covering over his face, languidly lounging in his comfortable chair, the only chair in the theater, smoking a cigar or, perhaps, with a purple drink.

The millionaire spoke to no one.

His go-between with the world was his butler, who paid his bills, arranged his entertainments, and was interviewed by the press, and so who, because of his peculiar relationship to the millionaire, also became famous.

One day an actor who was feeling very depressed because he had no work was sitting in the Waldorf Cafeteria reading a newspaper.

He happened to read a story about the eccentric millionaire and he realized—he was about the same height and build as this millionaire—he was about the same age—and he realized that if he could somehow kill the millionaire and take his place, why, it would be easy to impersonate this man who spoke to no one and wore a black covering over his face.

He was afraid of the butler, though.

So he studied from newspaper files and things the habits and characteristics of the butler and the millionaire.

One dark night he sneaked onto the grounds and by luck ran into the millionaire who was looking down an old well at the back of the house.

And so he hit the millionaire over the head and killed him.

It was dark by the well. He hurriedly got into the millionaire's clothes and put the black covering over his face and dumped the millionaire's body into the well and he noticed at the time that the body didn't make a splash.

So dressed, the impostor walked into the house, and into a life of ease and luxury.

And he found it was a cinch!

Because this butler was—a perfect butler.

He never had to give an order. The butler just knew what to do. The butler would bring him his breakfast, would run his bath, he arranged for him to have women, furnished him with cigarettes of hashish, ran the household, and planned all his fabulous entertainments.

His living was effortless.

And after a while he realized—no one could ever discover his identity. The scheme was perfect.

And he was right.

No one would ever discover his identity.

But this man's weakness was his conceit. You see, it never occurred to him that someone else might get the same idea he got. It never occurred to him that the man he killed was not the millionaire at all, but was an impostor, like himself, and that in a couple of months another impostor would come along and kill him, and that as a matter of fact, during the last few years there had been quite a few impostors, each with the same weakness, that same conceit.

No, no one ever knew of this—except the butler, of course, but he never told, because he likes his job.

The Santa Claus Murderer

❄   ❄
❄

ONCE upon a time there was a person who ended wars forever by murdering 42 Santa Clauses.

It all began about ten days before Christmas when a
Salvation Army Santa Claus was murdered midtown.

A morning newspaper carried the story, but the next day
five more Santa Clauses were murdered and it hit the head-
lines of every paper in the country.

Four of them were killed collecting money for the Salvation Army and the fifth was stabbed in the toy department
of Gimbels.

And people were outraged! They were indignant! They
thought what a monster, what a ghoul this guy must be, I
mean, to spoil the children's Christmas by murdering Santa
Claus.

They weren't concerned over the actual lives of the men
murdered, it was just what effect it would have on the children that upset everyone.

So the next day the town was filled with city and state
police, FBI men, and even some Naval Intelligence officers,
Treasury agents, and Department of Justice officials, all of
whom found excuses to get in on the case—and ten more
Santa Clauses were murdered, and the elusive killer wasn't
caught.

So that night all the working Santa Clauses held a secret
meeting to decide what to do.

They realized their responsibilities toward the children, but on the other hand it seemed sort of foolish to go out and just get popped off by this maniac.

And so one man, who was a brave man, and who had no dependents, volunteered to go out the next day in costume under heavily armed guard.

But his throat was slashed in his bed that night.

And so the next day there were no Santa Clauses in the city.

And people were all sort of irritable and jumpy, and kids were crying, and it just didn't seem like Christmas without the Santa Clauses.

But the next day some daffy Hollywood chick, some actress who wanted some publicity, came out dressed in a Mrs. Santa Claus costume.

And people and kids flocked around her, being the nearest thing to Santa Claus on the streets, and she got a lot of publicity, and she wasn't killed.

So the next day several more prominent women came out, all dressed up like Mrs. Santa Claus with white powdered hair and red skirts and pillows in their stomachs and Santa Claus hats, and they weren't killed either.

They decided maybe this maniac had stopped, so they sent out one Mr. Santa Claus as a test, but within an hour his body was being taken to Bellevue in an ambulance. There were three bullets in him.

And so Christmas that year was spent with Mrs. Santa Clauses.

And the next year the same thing started to happen all over again so they sent the women out immediately.

The next year the same thing happened; and the next, and the next—and year after year this patient and elusive maniac would kill any male dressed as Mr. Santa Claus, until finally, in the newspapers, in advertisements, and in people's minds, Santa Claus sort of dropped into the background and Mrs. Santa Claus became the central figure.

I mean Santa Claus was still there. He made the toys up at the North Pole and he was in charge of the elves, but it was Mrs. Santa Claus who rode the sleigh with the reindeer and slid down the chimney and gave away the presents and led the Christmas parade each year.

And the funny part of it was women really seemed to enjoy being Mrs. Santa Claus. No one had to pay them and it got to be such a fad that the streets around Christmastime were jammed with Mrs. Santa Clauses. And as time went by they began making little alterations in the traditional costume, first changing the shade of red, and then experimenting with entirely different colors, so finally each costume was unique and fantastic, beautifully colored, gorgeous.

It became a real honor to lead the Christmas parade.

And the kids loved it!

Christmas had never been like this before, with all these Mrs. Santa Clauses, and all the excitement, and gee!

But these kids, this new generation of children who grew up *believing* in Mrs. Santa Claus, were sort of different.

Because you see Santa Claus to very young children is— a god.

And about the time they stop believing in Santa Claus they start going to Sunday school and learning about a new God. And this new God doesn't just give them presents. He's sort of rough.

But all their lives they yearn for their old childhood god, their Santa Claus god.

Like witness their prayers, their saying—give me what I want.

But this new generation of kids who grew up believing in Mrs. Santa Claus seemed to have a different attitude toward women.

They began electing women to Congress and they elected a woman president and women mayors until pretty soon the country was entirely run by women.

They were mainly concerned with things like food, and there was much debate in Congress about various diets, and pretty soon even the poorest people had a lot to eat; and they were interested in houses, and soon, there was no housing shortage.

But there was one thing they wouldn't stand for.

They just weren't going to do it.

I mean what possible political reason could make these women send their guys out to get killed? It was ridiculous!

So with their political power and their financial power and the prestige of the United States they forced and encouraged other countries to let women run things.

So war was ended forever.

Men went on doing just what they'd always done. They worked in factories, and studied higher mathematics, and gambled on horses, and delivered the ice, and argued about philosophy.

But these arguments about philosophy didn't cause people to starve and kill each other.

And pretty soon all over the world, why—no one was hungry—everyone had nice houses—there was no more war —people began to be happy.

You know when you stop to think about it, a world revolution had taken place.

And gee, 42 Santa Clauses, that's not many people killed for a world revolution.

But the murderer, or really, the saint to whom humanity owed so much, who planned and carried out this almost bloodless revolution, was never caught and crucified.

Just went on living.

No, no one ever discovered the identity of this saint—that is—ahh—except me.

I know who the saint is.

Oh, I have no proof, but you see that's exactly why I'm so sure I know.

Because there is only one person capable of this, there is only one person with the genius, the daring, the imagination, the courage, the love of people, the blood lust, and patience required to carry out this greatest of all deeds.

That person is my little sister.

The Blond Bat

* *
*

Once upon a time a big blond bat sat down next to a bartender.

The bat had the most beautiful blue eyes the bartender had ever seen.

As they flew forty miles an hour on the Independent Subway, the bartender wondered if those baby blue eyes would glow in the dark like dull purple flames, like the blue light bulbs on the ends of the subway platforms.

Her costume was made of black velvet with silk black wings and satin gloves; she wore a curious mask which revealed more of her face than it hid; her shoes were high-heeled and furry, and he noticed her feet were delicate, and he wondered if she were barefoot underneath those shoes, or whether she wore stockings, and he bet she had beautiful toes.

This bartender was falling in love.

That was an odd performance, now! a bartender falling in love with a strange beautiful girl wearing a bat's costume on a subway.

Most subway loves get off at 34th Street to go into a railway station and thence to Saskatchewan—but it doesn't have to be that way.

For instance, in this story the bartender will not only have the courage to speak to this girl—they will even fall in love.

What! you say. You're a little indignant. You accuse me of sadism. To allow my character, the fat red-faced bartender to fall in love with this young girl. She will soon tire of him, you say, throw him off for a younger, more suitable man, for by the grandness and good taste of her costume and the dignity and grace of her features it's obvious she comes from a good family. How unhappy you're going to make the bartender! you say to me.

Fiddlesticks! I'm not going to make the bartender unhappy.

To be sure, though, the bartender will have many months of horror after this night of love and many years of sadness after that, but this is not unhappiness, for he will commit many kindnesses out of thankfulness to the world for allowing him his magic night.

No, unhappiness is something else; unhappiness is to be without the courage.

But back to the story: The train roared into the Delancey Street station and the bartender's eyes popped out of his head because hundreds of people in costume were dancing and singing and blowing horns and running and shouting and whoopeeing on the subway platform.

The girl got up.

The bartender also rose, and with eyes averted and distracted, he followed her out onto the subway platform and it was there he spoke to her.

She looked at him, startled; she looked him up and down; then she laughed, but she wasn't laughing at him, he could tell—it was a laugh of glee he was to remember.

She ran.

He chased her!

She ran through the crowd, she was slippery, she seemed

to glide between these mad gesticulating revelers while he had to fight for every foot, and in his passionate pursuit he stepped on Napoleon's toe, knocked over a shrieking fat witch, hit a clown in the stomach, sat a surprised gorilla down, tripped the queen of England, and on and on she ran, out of the subway down Delancey Street toward the river until finally he caught her and she rested quietly in his arms while she caught her breath, giggling occasionally with glee.

She was so soft he kissed her, and then they walked, arm-in-arm, watching the fireworks and the crowds, stopping, now and then, for a beer.

The whole town was having a party!

Everyone had a costume, everyone had a mask, and there were searchlights, confetti, and fireworks everywhere just like a marvelous Mardi Gras or something, and the bartender felt a little out of place with his drab street clothes and without even a mask.

But the girl said he was dressed fine.

And he asked her what all this celebrating was about, he hadn't heard of any celebration, but she just giggled and kissed him and that was that.

And so they struggled happily through the crowds and the night, stopping occasionally to dance to slow strange music in the taverns or the fiery jazz played on almost every corner.

She pointed at a big clock on a building. It was eleven o'clock.

She hurried him over to a long line that was walking slowly before a judges' stand, and when their turn came the judges made a big fuss over them, and one judge kept fingering the bartender's bright necktie admiringly, and so they won the contest, and both of them got big loving cups.

The judges ushered them up to a giant love seat built way up above the cheering crowd, a tremendous couch it was, bigger than a mattress.

This was their throne! They were king and queen of the night! They had won the costume contest.

Then the bartender heard a tremendous gonging.

The crowds began to shriek and scream.

He heard a siren long and low.

Delancey Street was mad.

His girl took off her mask and he held his breath, she was so beautiful as she pointed at the big clock on the building—she whispered to him, and soft with passion, lovingly she said—"It's midnight! Take off your mask!"

Chess

✳ ✳
✳

ONCE upon a time there was a demonstration of Russian courtesy.

There is a fair-sized city in Russia, the center of a great gray barren region.

In this town there is a chess club and anyone in the whole area at all seriously interested in chess belongs to this club.

For a number of years there had been two old men who were head and shoulders above all the rest of the club members. They weren't masters, but in this area they were the chief players, and for years the club members had been attempting to decide which of them was the better; each year there was a contest, and each year these two tied: First one would win, then the other, and then they would draw, or stalemate; the club was divided, half the members thought one was superior, half the other.

The club members wanted to have one champion.

So they decided this year to hold a different sort of contest: They decided to bring in an inferior player, an utterly unknown person from outside the area, and each of the candidates would play him a game, and they simply assumed each of the candidates would win against the mediocre player so there was no question of winning or losing; but rather they decided to vote afterward, after studying and discussing each of the candidates' games, and award the championship to him who played with better style.

The tournament evening arrived, and the first candidate played with the inferior player—until the inferior player finally shrugged his shoulders and said, "I concede. You obviously win." Whereupon the first candidate leaned over and turned the chessboard around, himself taking the position the inferior player had given up, and said, "Continue." They played longer until finally the inferior player was checkmated.

Then the second candidate played the inferior player until finally the outsider threw up his hands and said, "I concede." And the second candidate, exactly as the first candidate had done, turned the board around, and said, "Continue."

They played for a while until the harassed inferior player, looking blank, leaned back and shrugged his shoulders and said, "I don't know what to do. I don't know where to move. What should I do?"

The second candidate twisted his head around to get more of his opponent's view of the board, and then said tentatively, "Well, why don't you move *that* piece *there*." The outsider stared at the board uncomprehendingly, and finally shrugged his shoulders as if to say, "Well, it can't do any harm, and after all, what does it matter, as I know I'm going to lose anyway." With that gesture he moved the piece *there*.

The master frowned and pondered the board for several minutes before moving.

His frown deepened.

The corners of his mouth turned down.

His eyes hardened, he turned a sullen, stony, defiant stare at his audience for a moment before whispering in a choked voice all could hear, "I concede!"

He leaped up from his chair, raised his gold-headed cane quickly into the air, smashed it down onto the ebony and ivory chessboard, and split it in half.

He rushed from the room muttering loudly a long, strong string of profanities that were marvelous to hear.

He was, of course, awarded the club championship, and had, I think, incidentally demonstrated the proper way to lose a game.

The Monroe Street Monster

✳ ✳
✳

ONCE upon a time a monster moved into 91 Monroe Street.

That's a tenement block, full of Puerto Ricans and Italians, Jews and Negroes, Irish and some Chinese, many first generation immigrants, a lot of artists and bohemians; all these people wear costumes.

But this monster was very strange looking.

He was short and ugly and had bright carrot-red hair and was forty years old. He wore a long green cape which completely covered him; it dragged along the ground a little bit when he walked, so you couldn't see his legs.

This made him strange looking, but the thing which made people call him a monster was the peculiar way he walked—or rather, moved.

Because he didn't walk like ordinary people do.

He sort of glided.

It was like someone was pushing him on roller skates, or he was riding a one-wheeled bicycle, and some said he really sat cross-legged in the middle of the air, floating.

Some thought he was an angel, others thought he was a devil, but everyone, old ladies, young gangsters, and children alike, felt the same fear when they saw him coming, gliding.

People would rush inside to watch him from doorways and through windows, peeking at him from behind curtains, as he glided grimly down the vacated street.

It went on for about two weeks.

He had very regular hours. He went out early in the morning and returned early in the evening, and nobody ever knew where he went or what he did when he got into his apartment.

One evening as he turned down the block, and as the block emptied, a bum fell out of the bar at the other corner.

The bum began to stagger up the street toward the monster, and he was so drunk, swearing and lurching and talking to himself, he didn't notice the silence, or the emptiness, or the green-caped redhead moving quickly toward him.

But all of Monroe Street was watching.

They met.

The bum looked—and he saw the monster—and he reached in his pocket and brought out a cigarette, the cigarette was broken, and he said, "Hey buddy! You got a light?"

The monster fiddled around underneath his cape and brought out a match and lit the bum's cigarette.

It was at this point that the bum, who was so drunk, collapsed, and in falling, fell on top of the monster, knocking him down, knocking him into the middle of the street, and in the process, he grabbed onto the monster's cape and pulled it off.

The monster was completely exposed!

And the people rushed out and they formed a big circle around the monster and they just stared—!

And then someone said in a sort of disappointed voice, "Aww, he's only got three legs."

Then someone else said, "Yeah, he's no devil. He's no angel—hah! He's just got three legs. That's why he walks like that!"

Then they began to get angry with him, shouting at him belligerently for frightening them.

And the poor monster, there were tears rolling down his cheeks, as he tried to tell them that he didn't really mean to frighten them, it was just that he was ashamed of his deformity, that's why he wore the long cape.

Finally a guy stepped out of the crowd and helped the monster to his feet, and said, "Say, buddy, what you need's a drink!"

So the monster, cape over his arm, glided down to the bar at the corner, and a crowd of men followed him in.

His hands were shaking as he took his drink, so the other men pretended not to notice. One of them said, "You think the Yankees'll win tomorrow?"

Another said, "Well I got two bucks they will!"

The monster turned, pointing a steady finger at the man, shouting, "I'll take that bet!"

Because, you see, he was a Dodger fan.

That's really the end of the story.

But I can't help noticing that the monster and the people have completely forgotten the bum.

While they sit drinking and talking about baseball, the bum is unconscious in the gutter, and he'll never even know of this great deed he committed.

Kids are careful not to step on his body as they run back and forth chasing each other, but that's about the only attention he gets.

But—as the author—I have a certain power.

And so I'd like to express that gratitude which my characters failed to show. You see, this bum is going to die in a couple of months anyway of tuberculosis, but I'm going to have him picked up by the police on an alcoholic charge and they'll take him to Bellevue, and they'll discover his T.B. there, and they'll send him to a state sanitarium, to die. They'll take care of him.

The Language of Cats

※　　※
※

ONCE upon a time there was a gentleman.

He was a scientist. There were letters after his name.

He spoke a hundred languages from Iroquois to Esperanto.

He was the author of several little papers on astral mathematics.

He was thirty-five, authoritative, and quiet-spoken.

His hobby was playing chess on a three-dimensional board.

His job was the most dramatic known to scholarship, and the most hectic. He was hired by the armed forces to break codes and during the war had done brilliant work, going days without sleep. The generals were awed by him because several times, they said, he had literally saved the war by breaking the enemy's master codes. And indeed, that means he saved the world.

But for the life of him he couldn't remember to put cigarettes in ashtrays, so all the furniture was scarred with little brown burns.

His wife was blond and small and thin and was a very neat housekeeper.

He drove her to distraction.

He was constantly making messes all over the house, eating in the living room, leaving his socks in the middle of the floor, his shoes on the window sill; and flames, every once in a while, would burst from a wastepaper basket from an unextinguished butt, but luckily their house still stood.

He turned his wife into a nagger.

She'd shout at him ten times a day until finally he could stand it no longer; he could not, would not argue with her about such trivialities; his mind was filled with formulas and figures and strange words from ancient languages, and besides, he was a gentleman.

One day he left her. He packed his bags and moved into a cottage nearby in West Virginia with a Siamese cat.

2

The cat hypnotized him.

It was a beautiful blue-point Siamese. It talked a lot; that is, it meowed, meowed, meowed, meowed all the time.

He'd sit on his bed and stare at it for hours while it stalked cellophane balls, bounced from bed to dresser, then to the sink, to the floor, and then back again and again to the bed.

Every once in a while it would give the air a bat.

Suddenly it would stop and sleep.

He'd sit and stare at it, the pale gray, gently breathing ball of fur, and his thoughts would ramble over the dissatisfactions of his life.

Voltaire had once said he despised all professions which owed their sole existence to the spitefulness of men. Certainly his was such.

He had lost all interest in his friends, and women. He found most people shallow and vulgar.

Some evenings he made the rounds of the bars as if looking for someone, without the success, ever, of even getting drunk. Books put him to sleep.

And finally the cat became the center of his life, his sole companion.

One evening as he sat staring at it he developed a peculiar desire.

He wanted to communicate with it.

He decided to conduct some experiments.

So he lined the walls of his garage with a thousand little cages and placed a cat in every cage. Most of the cats he bought, others he just picked up off the street, and some he even stole from casual friends, so possessed was this scientist by his scheme.

On a tape recorder he began collecting all the cat sounds.

He recorded their howls of hunger, distinguishing those that wanted tuna fish from those that wanted salmon. Some wanted lung, liver, or fowl. And all these sounds he filed systematically in his growing record library.

He carefully compared the shriek when a *right* front foot was being amputated, to that made when a *left* front leg was being cut.

He recorded all the sounds they made when mating, fighting, dying, and giving birth.

Then he quit his government job and began to study in earnest the thousands of shrieks and caterwauls he had recorded, and after a while the sounds began to make sense.

Then he began to practice, mimicking his records until he mastered the basic vocabulary of the language.

Toward the end he practiced purring.

He had never experimented on his own cat. He wanted to surprise it.

One evening he walked into his apartment, hung his coat in the closet as usual, turned to his cat, and said, "MEOW!"

3

This was the way cats said "Good evening" when meeting.

But the cat did not seem surprised.

The cat answered, "Mrrrrowrow!" which meant, "It's about time!"

The cat gave him to understand that it would tutor him in the more complex subtleties of the language, that it was well informed of all his experiments, and that, if he did not pay attention to his lessons, the man would be Mrowr—sorry!

As the weeks went by, the man discovered to his continual amazement the fantastic intelligence of his Siamese cat.

Bit by bit he learned the history of the cats.

Thousands of years ago the cats had a tremendous civilization; they had a world government which worked perfectly; they had spaceships and had investigated the universe; they had great power plants that utilized an energy which was not atomic; they had no need of radios or television for they used some sort of mental telepathy; and some other wonders.

But one thing the cats discovered eventually was that the importance of any experience depended on the intensity with which it was felt.

They realized their civilization had grown too complex, so they decided to simplify their lives.

Of course they didn't want to just "go back to nature" —that would have been too much—so they created a race of robots to take care of them.

These robots were an improvement mechanically over anything nature had produced.

A couple of their greatest inventions were the "opposable thumb" and the "erect posture."

They didn't want to bother about fixing the robots when they broke down so they gave them an elementary intelligence and the power to reproduce.

Of course, we are the robots to which the cat referred.

And now the scientist understood why cats had always seemed so contemptuous of their masters.

The cat explained that cats were not afraid of death; indeed they led constantly passionate and heroic lives, and when properly prepared, when their time came, they welcomed death.

But they did not want *an atomic death.*

And the robots had developed a mean and irrational attitude toward *mice.*

"It occurred to us to merely wipe the race out, but then we'd have to go to all the trouble of making a new one," said the cat (in his own way, of course), "so we decided to try a thing which, frankly, many cats thought would be impossible—*to wit*: teaching a robot how to talk cat language so he could transmit our orders to the world!

"We chose you," said the cat in a condescending way, as perhaps our scientists would speak to a monkey whom they had taught to talk, "because of all the robots you seemed most promising and receptive and the foremost authority in your little field."

The cat gave the man a list of rules which he copied on a slip of paper.

The rules were:

DO NOT KICK CATS
NO ATOMIC WARS
NO MOUSETRAPS
KILL THE DOGS

"If the world does not obey these rules, we will simply eliminate the race," said the cat, and then closed his eyes and yawned and stretched and promptly went to sleep.

"Wait a minute! Wake up! Please!" pleaded the man timidly, touching the cat on the forehead.

"Let me sleep!" growled the cat. "You have your job. Get going!"

"But I can't just take these rules to people and say some cat told me. Nobody would believe me!"

The cat frowned and said, "Suppose we give you a little demonstration of our power? Then people will believe this isn't just a joke. A week from today I'll have some cats go through Moscow and Washington spraying a gas which will drive everybody insane for twenty-four hours. The gas will release all their destructive impulses. They won't hurt each other, but they will destroy everything they can get their hands on, all the buildings, bridges, public works, all the documents, and even all their clothes."

Then the cat yawned again, and went back to sleep.

The man, with the slip of rules in his hand, walked out into the streets to do as he had been told, but first, and he hardly knew what he was doing, strange mischief lit his eyes as he thought of his neighbors. He opened the thousand cages.

4

An October breeze hit him in the face, flame-colored

leaves crunched beneath his feet, the setting sun reddened
everything with its final gorgeous rays, the street noises
rushed into his ears as in a dream, and a Good Humor bell
was tinkling pathetically at the approach of the black night
and of winter, or so it seemed to him as he walked, dazed
by the tremendous responsibility he had been given, his
mind whirling in great circles, desperately finding poetry
and beauty in the cracks on the sidewalk, in the stripes on
the barbershop poles, in the snatches of young girls' con-
versations which he heard as he passed by them, in the out-
rageous odors of garbage cans, in the whole of the city
scene which he had never really noticed, had walked
through blindly before, his eyes turned inward on his work,
but which now he gulped in with gladdened earnestness—
but to escape! to escape his fantastic duty to the world he
lost himself in all its beauties; but this new world he saw
was seen by others, I'm sure, who were in very different
situations, and as it is this strange world he *saw* which I am
trying to describe, I shall digress a moment: Imagine a child
in England, a couple of centuries ago who had stolen a loaf
of bread or a handkerchief or a half-crown and whom
some stern and stupid judge had sent to prison, to grow
into manhood in prison, never knowing the softness of a
woman, never knowing a meal given with love, or never
tasting candy, never seeing a show, or any of our most
common pleasures—on his release we can easily imagine his
awe, delight, and terror, his great yearning to touch each
girl he meets, his need for patient love and endless explan-
ations (for he would understand almost nothing of our free
world) and that, not finding a person with such patience,
he would soon be back in prison—but all that's beside the
point—the point is that the world of this scientist escaping

his responsibility and the world of the young man just rudely vomited from a prison would *look* the same; and so to understand how this October night appeared through his daze and confusion—imagine how the world would appear to a person after finishing such a ridiculously lengthy, pointless sentence.

5

The lights began to twinkle on as the darkness descended.

A cream-colored convertible, in which four drunken high school boys were singing happily and shouting lustily at pedestrians, suddenly swerved off the road and cut the top off a fire hydrant, threw two of the boys through a jewelry store window, threw one of them twenty feet into the air so he landed flatly on his back on the pavement, and left the other, the only survivor, moaning miserably with broken ribs against the steering wheel; flames burst from under the hood of the twisted wreck which had stopped abruptly over the broken hydrant; the gushing water drenched the back of the car, but left the flaming front untouched.

An excited crowd began to gather around the catastrophe, hungrily devouring the spectacle.

The scientist, who was on the other side of the street, a witness to the whole accident, saw it as if it were a movie accident, and continued his aimless dreamy meandering; and he was clutching the slip of rules tightly in his fist, though he was not even aware of it, so lost was he in the beautiful movements, lights, and noises of the city.

Though he still walked, his mind turned itself inward

again, and he wondered whom on earth he could take these rules to—he didn't know the President, and anyone in authority to whom he spoke would certainly laugh.

He pondered the problem for a long time.

He looked out at the world again and discovered to his surprise that he was in front of his old house.

The lights were on. He had not communicated with his wife since the day he had left. He walked down the narrow path and entered the house without knocking, from habit, as he had always done.

His wife had her hat on.

"You get out of here!" she screamed. "I have a date! I don't ever want to see you again!"

The scientist looked around at his old house. Everything was the same. The furniture was even arranged in the same precise, neat way.

The furniture! It was this furniture that had been the cause of their breaking up. She had loved her furniture more than she had loved him.

He picked up a vase. She loved this vase more than she had loved him. He threw it against the wall.

Smash!

His wife screamed.

Next this antique chair of which she was so fond.

Smash!

It broke into three pieces.

He threw the lamp out the window.

Crash!

"Stop it!" screamed his wife. "Are you crazy?"

He went into the kitchen and got a knife, throwing some ashtrays on the floor and tipping over the bookcase on the way, and began to rip the overstuffed chairs.

"Stop it! Stop it!" screamed his wife, now hysterical and weeping.

But the scientist hardly heard her. He was ripping, smashing, tearing, destroying utterly, utterly demolishing, in a frenzy of rage more overpowering than her tears, every piece of furniture in the house.

Then he stopped.

And she stopped crying.

Their eyes met and they fell toward each other, in love more than ever before.

The violent scene had somehow changed them both. The man's eyes were now clear and his brow had lost its heaviness. Her voice was soft and warm.

Then the man remembered the cats, and what they were going to do.

"Look!" said her husband, pressing his foot on the gas, out of Washington for a while. Let's go on a second honeymoon. Let's take the car and go out west to the mountains and just get away from everybody and everything. We'll find some wilderness and live there. Now don't ask any questions. Just do as I say."

She did as he said, and an hour later they were driving westward out of Washington.

"Darling!" said his wife suddenly. "We'll have to go back!"

"Why?"

"Didn't you have a Siamese cat in your cottage? He'll starve. You can't just leave him locked in there. And if we go back you can pick up some of your clothes. It seems silly to buy new ones when all we have to do is go back to the cottage."

"Look!" said her husband, pressing his foot on the gas, speeding the car perceptibly. "That cat can take care of itself!"

6

Driving in shifts it took them three and a half days to reach the edge of the mountains, where they bought a rifle, knapsacks, sleeping bags, cooking utensils, and all the paraphernalia they would need to live away from civilization for a while. They began their journey on foot, sweating and groaning under the weight of their knapsacks.

They did not see another human being for a couple of months.

But once, when they were walking a short distance from their camp, they met a wildcat.

The wildcat snarled menacingly.

The man had left his rifle at the camp.

The wildcat was between them and their camp.

So the scientist pushed his wife behind him and began to snarl and meerrrooowww.

For several minutes they spoke, and then the wildcat turned and ran off.

"Darling, what were you doing? You sounded as if you were actually talking to that wildcat."

And so the man told her the whole story of how he had learned to speak the language of the cats, and that now probably Washington and Moscow were in ruins, and soon the whole human race would be destroyed.

He explained that it had just been too much. The human race was not worth it. And so he had decided to get away from everything and get what little happiness he could out of these last few remaining days.

"I have no idea how or when the cats will destroy us, but they will, for they have powers we could never imagine," and his voice trailed off in sorrow. She took his hand and they walked slowly to their camp.

Now she understood his flashing eyes, and this new energy he'd gotten, his new youthfulness—his madness was becoming apparent to her—and she found it strange that, even so, she loved him more now than ever before.

7

A couple of weeks later they were sitting around their campfire. Snow surrounded them, and while the scientist stared silently at the stars, the woman grew cold, and began to shiver. Finally she got up and began to pace back and forth.

"What date is today?"

"I don't know," answered the man absently.

"It must be around Christmas," she said.

The man glanced at her sharply, and then grew thoughtful. A few minutes later he leaped to his feet and shouted. "What was that? I heard sounds!"

His wife listened for a moment, and answered, "I didn't hear anything."

"Listen! There it is again! It's like horses' hooves!"

"But darling. I don't hear anything."

"Well, I'm going out and see who it is!" said her husband determinedly.

And he walked out into the blackness.

His wife heard him talking, loudly, as if to someone, but she heard no other voices. She called out to him, "Darling, who's out there? Who are you talking to?"

He shouted back, "Oh, it's all right. It's just Santa Claus, those were his reindeer we heard."

His wife said sadly to herself, "There's no point in telling him there is no Santa Claus."

8

He came back with a green plant, a cactus, which he had obviously just picked from the snow, and with a grand, old-world bow, handed it to her, saying, "Santa Claus gave this to me to give to you for your Christmas present. He came all the way out here, just so you wouldn't spend Christmas without a present."

She took the plant in her hands and moved nearer the the fire. These bursts of madness frightened her, or was he joking? Or was he being gallant? She looked up at him, staring out across the mountain ranges again, at those far-away stars. How noble and insane he looked. But then terror touched her again, and she said, rather timidly, "You know, dear, back there at the house—when you got so angry —it was very good of you not to hit me."

He looked over at her a moment, a little annoyed, but he was silent, and returned his gaze to the horizon.

"But then," she added, "I needn't have worried. You're such a gentleman."

9

They returned to civilization shortly after that.

Moscow and Washington were not in ruins.

And, much to his wife's surprise, it turned out her husband was not insane—the lunatic was that Siamese cat. They discovered the cat's corpse at the cottage—dead from starvation.

For there is a language of the cats, but all Siamese cats are crazy—always talking about mental telepathy, cosmic powers, fabulous treasures, spaceships, and great civilizations of the past, but it's all just meowing—they are impotent —just meows!

Meows!

Meows!

Meows!

Meows!

Meows. . . .

10,000 Reflections

✱　✱
✱

A HUNDRED feet up in the air the great crystal chandelier was flashing with the light of five hundred candles nestled in its glass.

Five hundred flames tossing, reflected ten thousand times.

The rude guests were aghast at the glittering giant—for the hall below was filled with peasants—it is 1789, it is July 14, the French Revolution is on!

This is the great dining hall of the Duke, his dinner guests have been stabbed in their chairs, and while their corpses sit still at their table, the peasants eat—grabbing fistsful of cake —gobbling it.

As the dining hall filled with the riffraff, ravenous, as it became chock-full with hysterical murderers—all waving blades and clubs and shrieking with freedom and passion— the great chandelier began to tinkle.

Now it is an awesome sound to hear ten thousand finely cut pieces of crystal begin to rub shoulders, and the acoustics in the room were good.

It was as if someone had begun to ring a million glass bells all at once.

The tinkle cut through every shriek.

The sweating throng grew quiet.

All eyes fastened themselves in wonder on the thing, all faces were turned up, aghast at the trembling splendor, and to a man—terror-struck.

It was almost imperceptible at first—the sound of deep sighs in the silence around the tinkling; just as imperceptibly the chandelier had begun—this way and that, back and forth, on the cast-iron chain on which it hung—the chandelier began to swing.

The room became filled with the sounds of sighs as they all saw it moving in the arc of the pendulum.

Then the sighs ceased.

The pendulum swung—it swung faster now, each time its arc grew wider, its five hundred flames were bent flat, first this way, then that, as it raced through the air, increasing its speed.

The nature of the tinkle changed: in gaining momentum the tinkling grows silent as the chandelier plunges on its path, but on the end of each swing the tinkle returns, a crescendo of glass, a hundred times louder!

But in the silence of the swing a tiny voice can now be heard.

It is the tiny sound of sobbing, of wanton weeping, it is the tiny voice of grief.

It is the voice of an angel, and it seems to come from the very center of the air above their heads.

Every member of the mob is a statue, face upturned, eyes closed, breathing deeply in perfect time with the swinging light, hypnotized.

Here is a perfect example of mass hypnosis. They are all unconscious, deeply asleep.

They'll stand here like this until the sunlight wakens them at dawn, but their memories will be all confused, and they'll never have any idea what was happening on this night; they hear no tears, nor how the childish shriek of grief turns into the rage of revenge in each crescendo.

The pendulum swings faster.

The room suddenly darkens as most of the candles blow out, and on the next swing the room was plunged into a pitch blackness, utterly lightless, and at that moment the five-year-old daughter of the Duke lost her grip on the cast-iron chain of the chandelier, which feverishly she had been pumping as yesterday she had her playground swing, and her grief-shaken body flew through the air, from the dead light was flung, through the blackness, pitched over their heads.

Miss Lady

*   *
*

Once upon a time a sad little girl walked along a summer road.

She was about three years old, and she was crying because her brother was walking so fast she couldn't keep up, and then she stumbled, in a cloud of dust.

Her brother heard her cry but he kept on walking faster and faster and faster.

She was alone.

She looked over and saw a cottage and there was a man watching her from a window, peeping at her from behind a thick curtain, so she waved.

The face disappeared.

She walked to the back of the house, and there was another face, at another window, peeping out. She waved again.

And that face disappeared.

She climbed up on the back porch and knocked on the screen door, and after a few minutes the door opened a little. She walked in.

There were some men, and they gave her a Coca-cola, and she talked with them, explaining about her sunburn, about her brother, and something about a trip to Canada her mother and father were going to take, and the men listened to her earnestly.

She hit one of them!

He picked her up and swung her through the air and she screamed! Then he perched her on his shoulder and she held his head tightly afraid of falling, but then she lost her fear and just sat there, and they all laughed at her.

So she asked for another Coca-cola.

One of the men got it for her and she insisted on drinking it out of the bottle; she sat on one of the guys' laps and listened, while the men talked of other things, taking great slugs of Coca-cola occasionally.

Then she began prattling again and the men all stopped to listen to her. She asked one of them to fix her dirty stringy hair ribbon.

She played quite the lady and the men spoke to her with exaggerated English accents and this was wonderful!

Then she pulled one of them down on the floor and got up on his back and rode him like a horse, shouting gidiyap! gidiyap! gidiyap!

Wow!

The little girl asked if she could come and live with them, and the men said sure!

So the men and the little girl got into a car and drove to Florida.

You see, these men were bank robbers.

The little girl loved it! She lived with them for eight months. She played on the beach with them, swam in the ocean, ate in big restaurants, lived in the best hotels, even drank champagne once! And she had a pretty maid who did nothing but wait on her and help her buy white dresses and orange bathing suits and all the toys little girls need.

They were always buying her presents and she loved them very much, but one day she got homesick and began crying for her brother and her mother and her father.

The gangsters were very unhappy but they bought her a ticket to her little hometown and they saw her off on the train. The conductor assured them she would arrive safely, which she did.

The police searched Florida for the bank robbers but they had flown to far corners of the globe.

The little girl continued her life with her family in the little town. She went to school. Much later she went to college; as a matter of fact, she attended Vassar.

2

Now she is a prostitute in Buenos Aires.

She is lying on a couch and her eyes are red from marijuana. Her clothes are lying on a chair. A sailor heavy-footedly leaves her room. She is so sad. Look! There is a tear on her cheek. Smoke is in her eye. What a rare tear.

She is so pretty!

I can't help liking her. Because I know her secret, her quest, and why she lives this way.

I know she's looking for them.

The Man Who Was
Always Wishing

*   *
    *

ONCE upon a time there was a man who was always wishing for things.

He'd wish for things like there'd be no more wars, or
people everywhere wouldn't starve anymore, and then
sometimes he'd wish he had a million dollars or magical
powers, so he could change all the misery around.

But he didn't do anything except wish for things.

He was a bum.

One day a bartender asked him, he said, "Look here,
why do you make all these fantastic wishes? I mean if you
want to end wars, why don't you go into politics and do
something about it? Or if you want a million dollars, why,
man, go out and earn it! Or at least, if you have to wish for
things, why don't you wish for something you can possibly
get? You know these fantastic wishes are never going to
come true."

And the bum explained himself this way, he said, "Look
here, a man goes through life wishing for many things,
and some of our wishes come true, and some don't—but
no man lives his whole life without ever having a wish
come true. I mean God must grant every man at least one
wish during his lifetime. But you ordinary people! You
make so many petty wishes. You wish you had five dollars

to buy this or that, or you wish you had this girl or that one, why, it's easy for God to grant one of your wishes. But look at me on the other hand. I have never made an ordinary wish!

"Do you understand?

"When God gets around to answering one of my wishes he's going to have some trouble. You're going to see a lot of changes around here when God gets around to answering one of my wishes, because do you understand? *I have never made an ordinary wish!*"

Well.

The bum grew older, forty, fifty, and sickly and skinny because of the way he was living, and still none of his fantastic wishes had come true.

One day he happened to wander into the zoo.

And he began watching the giraffes, which were in a large cage by themselves near the edge of the zoo, so they had a lot of room.

He watched them galloping around swinging their big necks to and fro like ponderous dancing.

He realized that this was the most beautiful thing he'd ever seen.

But something was wrong.

He couldn't figure out what it was. At first he thought it was the fact that the animals were caged that somehow spoiled this almost perfect scene, but the cage was landscaped just like a regular jungle scene with rocks and little trees and things, so he decided this couldn't be it.

Then it hit him!

It was the fact that the giraffes were so big, they were out of proportion to everything else.

They seemed out of place.

He noticed some flowers growing in the cage and he thought—wouldn't it be great if the flowers were giant. He wished that the flowers were tall.

Then he got dizzy, and he put his hand over his eyes, and the dizziness went away, and then he looked and—

There they were!

The flowers were tremendous! eighteen feet tall, and the giraffes were running around among them, batting the big flowers with their necks, sticking their noses into the morning-glories, and the perfume! the perfume filled the air; and colors! the great green stalks, purples, reds, and oranges of the blossoms sprung among the brown and yellow spotted careening giants, stunned him; and then all the giraffes began to lick the flowers from which they seemed to get some substance, their tongues flickering like pink fish, and he watched them one by one drop to the ground, their eyes drooping, and closing, until finally all lay asleep.

It was even more beautiful than he'd imagined.

His wish had been answered.

His wish had been answered!

And—I mean—well—the giraffes and the flowers were nice, they were really very pretty, but—this was nothing like no more war, or people everywhere never have to starve anymore, or Christ! he didn't even get a million dollars.

And he wondered what to do now. He'd never learned a trade or made any real friends, and he realized there was nothing he could do. His life had no meaning now.

He was drinking a bottle of orange pop, and he broke it against the bars of the cage like he'd seen someone do in a Hollywood movie, and very methodically he cut his wrists.

And then for some reason he kneeled down and slashed

his ankles and lay down on the grass with his arms stretched out like a man on a cross, to die.

As he lay there dying he reflected that God had been rather mean. Here he'd been so faithful to his belief, never wished for food when he was starving, or a lover when he was lonely—and he'd been so lonely. He felt cheated, as if God had taken advantage of him. He felt somehow that God hadn't been a very good sport.

But a few minutes before he died he happened to glance back at the rest of the zoo, at the rest of the world.

He leaped to his feet, shocked! at what he saw.

For he saw that God hadn't answered his wish at all.

And he realized that had he not taken his own life God would have granted one of his great wishes, because He hadn't made the flowers giant. He'd merely made the cage, the giraffes—and the man, very small.

A Following

＊　　＊

＊

A LITTLE girl walks behind her brother on the way to school.

As they pass a huge red house a little girl dressed beautifully in blue starched bows appears from behind a bush and joins her, falling in step behind him.

From a yellow brick house down the driveway comes running another tot, whose elegant dress is as gray as the clouds that overhang the luminous country this morning.

Down the block they are joined by two more girls, each popping out from behind a fence or tree after he had passed, and as he does not glance back at his sister once, each of them is, by him, unseen.

Now another jumps out and joins them.

They are each seven years old. He is eleven.

He takes from his pocket a ball, and begins to bounce it as he walks.

They each do the same.

They are quiet as mice. Each bounces a ball, each walks like he walks.

For no reason he leaps, as if leaping over a stream.

The six little girls do the same.

By them, *unseen*, but playing their game, behind them all comes another, a foreigner, a fifty-year-old bouncing a tennis ball, whose face is as gray as the tennis ball, to whom the day is not luminous, but flat, dreary, dank and dark, who sees in their homes naught but vulgar opulence, who has seen war, famine and the horror in the camps, who is sought even now by Israeli secret police, who limps slightly —Oh! if that story were told.

Now like the leader, for no reason, he leaps.

It is the eccentric, new truant officer.

On Hope

*
*   *
*

THE monkey leaped on the man's shoulder.

The man shuddered for he knew who it was. He knew exactly which monkey of the ten thousand that roam about on the Rock of Gibraltar, tame and free as pigeons, walking around in the parks and streets.

It was a demon monkey.

It was the one he'd trained to bring him necklaces, who brought him pearls, garnets, and amber from moonlit bedrooms in the big hotels—from women sunk in snoring.

The monkey dangled before his eyes the largest diamond in the world.

The whole thing began several days previously when all on Gibraltar went into an uproar. The Rock of Gibraltar was visited by royalty, by the queen mother, and the princess. A battleship brought them and their entourage, and with them the famous necklace, the largest stone of which was the *Diamond of Hope*, which the princess was to wear at some great state occasion. (There's a curse on the necklace, you know, and misfortune had followed it, and come to whomever possessed it until it became part of the British crown jewels in the middle of the nineteenth century.)

On the very first night the royal party was in, the monkey returned to his gypsy master with the necklace. The necklace, of course, was valueless. It couldn't possibly be sold. Gibraltar would be swarming with police searching for it.

The gypsy was annoyed with the monkey, irritated at its genius, and terrified of being caught by the police with the gems; and besides, although he had no particular regard for the government—(being a gypsy) he liked the idea of "the princess" and wouldn't dream of stealing her necklace. So he quickly wrapped it up and addressed the package to her and dropped it in an ordinary mailbox. He enclosed a note to her saying something like, "You really ought to guard this more carefully."

The next night the monkey returned again with the necklace.

This time his note implored her to have the police guard the necklace more carefully, and he even gave them advice. He advised them to place the necklace in the center of a cage.

(For a monkey of course couldn't get into a locked cage.)

Then the third night, when this story begins, the monkey again brought the gypsy the necklace, and fell at the gypsy's feet, dead. Shot. Very probably the monkey had been fatally wounded by a guard as he was escaping.

The gypsy shuddered at the diamond, and was not surprised at the death of his friend.

The first two times it had been like some freak occurrence, like a weird accident—to unexpectedly discover oneself in possession of part of the British crown jewels! but now . . .

When he received the gems for the third time the whole thing was plunged into meaning. It no longer seemed like an accident. He had been given the necklace. Fate was at work. Now, the necklace was his.

He put it in his pocket.

It never occurred to him (being a gypsy) to doubt the reality of the curse which accompanied the diamond, and he accepted his fate with the stone. Quietly and secretly he buried the animal.

And as he thought about it he was actually a little pleased that he, a gypsy, had been singled out by fate to take the curse off the princess, and the English throne.

He walked down to the shore of the Mediterranean and took off his clothes, and—having nothing in which to put the necklace, he put it on—dove in, and swam.

There was a full moon and the sea was perfectly calm.

Just off Gibraltar there's a very deep place in the Mediterranean. It's called the Gibraltar Trench. Only a mile from shore the sea is a mile deep.

The gypsy was a very good swimmer.

He swam out a mile, over this spot, took the necklace off and dropped it.

At that moment a smile lit his face as he imagined the thousands of Sherlock Holmes' searching for it for the next fifty years.

The man lazily began to swim back toward shore, and the necklace fell down into the depths.

They each had a mile to go—the man had a mile to swim, and the gems had a mile to fall.

The necklace fell much faster than the gypsy swam.

It fell straight down until it got about a hundred feet from the bottom, where it came to rest on the dorsal fin of a shark.

The shark had been sleeping, but the necklace woke it, and it turned round and around wondering what was happening. It decided to go up to investigate.

The shark swam upward even faster than the necklace had fallen.

Meanwhile the man still lazily swam toward the huge "rock," now ablaze as never before with the royal festivities, with a million electric light bulbs—and he thought of the curse. The stone would never bring its misfortune to anyone ever again; it was finished forever, its power over man extinguished for good, buried beneath a mile of water.

The he looked over his shoulder and saw the necklace floating a foot above the water, moving slowly past him.

(The gypsy did not see the shark's fin, he only saw the necklace glittering in the moonlight, as if floating in the air, not coming toward him, but moving past him, now receding into the distance.)

The man immediately realized that one of two things were true. Obviously, either he was witnessing a miracle (and the whole thing smacked of the miraculous) or, he was having a hallucination.

He decided to find out.

Was it a miracle? or, was it a delusion?

He began to shout and wave his arms and splash, and he began to swim after the necklace.

And sure enough the necklace stopped and after a moment began to move toward the man.

The man is swimming toward the necklace. The necklace is moving toward the man.

That is where the story ends.

However, I can't help noticing, at this moment, that at first glance it seems inevitable—you know, that the shark will devour the man.

But I do not believe that result is as inevitable as it seems at first glance; that is, I believe there are several reasons, so to speak, for hope.

1. I do not think a shark has ever been approached like this before, that is, by a man wondering whether the shark is a miraculous manifestation, or whether it is merely a figment of his own imagination.

2. The man is a gypsy animal trainer.

3. The shark is now in possession of the necklace.

The One Come

❋   ❋
❋

ENCRUSTED with colonnades and bright steeples the little southwestern town looked from the mountain as if it were an Early American engraving.

Sheet lightning flickered in the sunset.

There was a chimney below from which red smoke poured, and another loosed a long black line which curved over the valley; the orange forge glimmered in the twilight.

It was as if a churchbell should ring.

All the birds were quiet.

The dark pool offered an unmoving reflection of still twigs, and later, of a million stars among the black somber hunks of trees.

All the fireflies were quiet.

This pool was as if a suicide had stayed in its sludge, its skull a nest of salamanders.

It was as if some haunting were going on.

In the town there was a cheery brightness from each window and the light absolutely streamed out of them, illuminating the shrubs and silent squares of lawn; as one would move on down into the squalid sections where the children were still out playing in the streets, the lighting changed, the windows were grimier, narrower, the shades more frequently drawn, and the streetlamps were without

frosted glass, but bulbly glared, casting ghastily a blacker
shade.

Along an unlit lane at last at the farthest edge, not too
distant from the city dump (on one's right might be a deep
ditch) there would be the odor floating in the darkness of
garbage cans in the tall grass, of wild daisies, dandelions,
and marvelous weeds, and of grease. . . .

Old stars are the only light, and they aren't much help.
The stars were great as guides on grander journeys over
oceans to discover continents, but when one's problem is
immediately not to trip in ruts of uncared-for roads . . .

A giant cloud begins to cross the sky.
Now there is no light . . . whatsoever.
A moment's light!
Lightning.
There was a turn ahead and if that flashing moment's
image were correct, one should begin right here the veer,
and the ground should begin right here—ah . . . yes it does!
to rise as I round the corner.
Flash!
The thunder threw my senses into a keener pitch, and
memories of a mad music and the sunlight of that Monday
morning, and the memory of her mood, and the mangle of
her muscles twisting in the pool.
Crash!
A tree burst into flames in back of me, and there is the
ozone smell of the fiery fork which missed me by a hundred yards back there, but the sharp CRACK! which
seemed to explode almost inside my head moves me for-
ward now in a faster race, and all obstacles vanish under-

foot, and there's no question of falling to caution my motion, for I move in a miraculous balance.

I blink like a banshee in the blast of water, like the banshee—I am, in the great gush I grin, and just as whirling rain turns rut to mush, I begin.

I am the one come to avenge suicides.

The Mirror Story

※　※
※

ONCE upon a time there was a poet who wanted to turn his brains into money.

He was a good poet.

He was devoted to his profession, to the craft of his field, with his whole being.

He was well-educated, or at least, well-read; and he had a fine imagination, and could be eloquent—when writing—but he didn't know how to talk to people; he was shy, and he always had the feeling that people were relating their words to something that he didn't understand.

As he was a real poet it, of course, means that he must work at menial jobs—restaurant work, clerk jobs, messenger jobs.

There is no way a true poet can earn money by his work.

One day he looked around—and he saw all these morons, these vulgar, criminal, immoral, stupid, dull, all these idiots —all of whom can earn a living!

And he figured there must be some way a person of his intelligence could figure out so as not to have to work at these ridiculous jobs.

So he borrowed a black leotard from a dancer friend, and got a heavy black piece of cloth which he put over his head like a monk's cowl, and he got an oval piece of glass, just a little larger than a face, which he put in front of his face under the cowl; but it was not regular glass, it was what's called one-way glass; that is, it was the kind of glass that when you look through it one way it's clear, transparent glass, but when you look at the other side it's a mirror; he put this glass in front of his face so that he could see out, but anyone who looked at him saw only his own reflection.

He went to a Greenwich Village nightclub and got a job as an oracle.

A fortuneteller.

He had a little table in the nightclub, and he'd sit there, and people would come and ask him questions of the sort one asks an oracle, about the future, and he'd just say anything that came into his head. He'd make up nonsense, speak gibberish, quote lines of other people's poetry, and he had a good imagination so he'd make up little fantasies, stories, and people seemed to like it.

He discovered that when he had his mirror on he lost his shyness.

He could talk to people easily.

Some people even took him seriously, but he just laughed at them, and never pretended to be anything other than an entertainer.

After a while, he found he was earning a good living at the nightclub.

There was a girl, a striptease dancer, who also worked at the nightclub.

She worked under black light.

Ultraviolet light.

But only her costume was luminous, she wasn't, and as there was no other light, as she did her dance, as one by one her clothes dropped off, she disappeared.

Only her clothes were luminous, so when the last bra or panty dropped, she was invisible, and the stage was left littered with luminous blotches of clothing.

That was her act.

They fall in love.

But the poet when he doesn't have his mirror on is still his same old shy self. He doesn't know how to approach the girl, and doesn't know that she's also interested in him.

One evening (it's the middle of the week, business is slow) he sees the girl walking across the empty dance floor toward him, and she's holding something behind her back, so he can't see what it is.

She sits down at his table, and . . .

Wow! Here she is!

And he has his costume on, his mirror on, so suddenly he can talk!

He's just about to express himself, to express his love—when the girl says, "Look! I don't want my fortune told. I don't want to know about myself. I want to know about you!"

And at that point she took from behind her back an oval mirror from her dressing table, just a little larger than a face, and she held it up in front of his face-mirror, and said, "What do you see?"

Excuse me, my reader, but I must digress a moment to explain what he would see: You know when you stand between two mirrors, or when you sit in a barber chair, there seems to be a passageway in the mirrors; but if you ever stop to notice you'll observe that, though you can see perhaps six or seven levels in, you can never see to the end of the passageway; always your own first reflection gets in the way, and if you try to bend out of the way the whole passage bends out of the mirror frame.

But in this case he would see out of the glass and see a mirror, but the mirror would "see," so to speak, only a mirror, which would in turn see a mirror, and et cetera.

There would be nothing in between the mirrors to block the view so he would see the passageway going straight out to infinity.

So to recap the situation: The girl whom he loves is sitting in front of him, and he has his mirror on, so he can speak, and he is just about to express his love when the striptease dancer says, "What do you see?" And at that moment the girl vanishes, the nightclub vanishes, and the man sees a passage to infinity.

He doesn't say anything.

The girl takes the mirror away, and says, "Say something!"

But the man doesn't say a word.

She tugs at his sleeve, and says, "Don't just sit there, say *something.* . . ."

But he doesn't move.

And for seventeen years he hasn't moved.

He still sits, exactly in that same position, a catatonic in a mental hospital—he's fed through a tube, and is incontinent, and has completely lost contact with the outside world.

But the doctors and nurses can tell—from changes in his facial expression, and from the words he mutters just inaudibly, so that they can never quite make out what he's saying—they can tell that he's leading an active life in his mind, in a dream world he is having experiences. . . .

And in this world of his dreams, in the life he leads inside his head—all the rest of the people are wearing mirrors over their faces, and only he doesn't have one.

He feels very much like an outsider because of this, and he tries to find out, he questions people—why doesn't he have a mirror over his face like the rest of them?

But people either give him very phony answers and try to con him, or they pretend they don't know what he's talking about.

And because of this he finds he has to get very menial jobs, like dishwashing jobs, clerk jobs, or messenger jobs.

As this "whole world" is, after all, just his imagination, as it's just his dream—why—anything can happen.

I mean there are any number of ways this story might end.

Anything can happen in a dream.

For instance: After working all week at some awful job he takes his whole pay check and goes to the drug addicts' den.

(No real drug, of course, just what he imagines a drug addicts' den is, for in a dream whatever you might think a drug addicts' den is like—that's the way it *really* is.)

But the other people at the drug addicts' den, when they got high, oh! they danced, and sang, and laughed, and had a wonderful time; but he never did, he would find a comfortable chair and just sit.

And as the years went by he became adjusted to his world. Actually, he forced out of his consciousness this knowledge which he has, that he is actually different from the rest of them, that he doesn't have a mirror over his face. Whenever anyone would make any allusion to this fact, he would pretend not to hear, or he would pretend that they were talking about something else. And as the years go by he grows to think of himself as "normal." You know, everyone's a little neurotic, everybody has problems. But he grew to think of himself as just another ordinary human being—although—there are times when he does suspect, there are times when he does think that it's just a little peculiar that a person would go out and spend his whole pay check at the drug addicts' den, I mean—just to sit.

But there is another way this story might end, for instance: He meets a girl, and the girl also doesn't have a mirror over her face, and of course they recognize each other immediately, that is, that neither of them have mirrors in front of their faces.

And she tells him (she's been in "this world" longer than he) that he doesn't have to work at these awful jobs, and that she can show him how to get by. . . .

"Come to my house," she says. (Their relationship from the first becomes like a brother-and-sister relationship, rather than a sexual one.)

And so they walk out of town down to the edge of the ocean, and they walk down the beach for maybe a mile to a very isolated spot where there are no people; there's a very pleasant grove of palm trees, and in the center of the grove there is a small tent.

"See!" she says, "I live here. I don't have to pay any rent. I go swimming every morning. It's healthy living in the sun. It's wonderful."

"Well, yes," says the man, "It's great—but how do you eat?"

"I'm just about to fix lunch now. Why don't you stay and have lunch with me?"

And so she spreads a blanket out on the sand, and gets two tin pie plates, and goes down to the edge of the ocean, and he watches her down there, gathering things from the surf and placing them in the pie tins.

She returns and puts the plates down on the blanket and they sit down cross-legged on the sand and she begins to eat.

He looks down at his plate and there in the center is a little pile of pebbles, little pebbles worn round and smooth by the ocean.

He picked one up and examined it—it was really just a stone.

He put one of them in his mouth, and made a little face, gulped—and swallowed it.

She said, "It's a little difficult at first, but you get used to it after a while."

There is another way this story could end, but that ending's pornographic, and I don't write those kinds of things.

Pornography has no place whatsoever in literature.

Fingernails

*   *

*

WHEN the Paris police surgeon operated on the dead woman he discovered her stomach filled with a cup of fingernails.

The apelike expression on the dead face, its ugly grin, set in gangrene, was photographed in color. The grotesque head, gross, horribly demonic, sporting bleached hair, had been attached unnaturally to the body of a teen-ager. And the ghastly surgery had been successful, for the older woman's head had lived two years on the youthful body.

In such operations the cortolon balance is invariably upset. (Cortolon is a substance which controls the growth of fingernails and toenails.) Either a patient's nails disappear entirely or, as in this case, nail growth frequently is speeded up to several inches a day.

She could have been immortal if she hadn't bitten her fingernails.

True Confessions Story

ONCE upon a time there was a real Henry James tea party.

It was a regular English weekend at the turn of the century. There was the great green lawn, and the terrace of white Italian marble onto which figured French doors opened revealing oaken gleams of furniture polish.

There on the lawn were a few mannered children quietly fingering their hoops and solemnly petting terriers, and their elders were scattered about chatting, grouped mostly on the marble.

But above the general chatter-level one voice was continuously recognizable by its queer, clear, cultivated pitch, and a certain forcefulness of tone. This dominant voice was punctuated by phrases from the Continent, and a twang ghostily edged it, cutting the surrounding buzzing.

This voice belonged to an American.

She was a society woman about seventy years old.

She was a mildly famous old woman of letters who had come to Europe at eighteen, and such were its enchantments and her successes, she had stayed. Years ago she'd published slim volumes entitled "LETTERS" which by chance had been written prophetically to the right people who by sterner work were to create a literary world of that age.

She'd ridden their wave.

Suddenly, and with a sort of squeak, the voice stopped.

This sudden ceasing signaled a slowly mounting silence which enveloped even the children on the lawn who turned curiously suspended toward the portico . . . the old lady walked stiffly toward the French doors, but with a trembling, and behind her in the white marble trailed a yellow stream of water.

As she reached the doorways one of the terriers began to bark shriekily.

The old lady turned on the still astounded groups.

"What do you mean embarrassing me like this!" she demanded. "I'm an old lady! I have kidney trouble! What do you mean by this vulgar show of silence! How dare you! I've never in all my life witnessed such vile taste!"

And she stomped angrily and disappeared into the mansion, and she decided then, right there, to go home.

After a decent interval ordering her affairs fanfarelessly she left Europe for good . . . for the Upper Peninsula of Michigan.

She was a different person when she arrived at the little town of her childhood.

She had taken off her girdles, her dresses darkened, and her hair was now snow-white, and instead of the perfectly groomed society woman, she appeared there the perfect picture of a nice old lady. She had come home to die.

The family home (it was always referred to as "the house") had been closed for years; the others in her family had died long ago; she was a sole survivor.

She decided it would be fun to fix the place up as it used to be, as it had been in her childhood.

So she hired carpenters.

And within a month she moved in, out of the town to the estate in the woods.

In the Upper Peninsula there exists a group of Indians who, since the Seminoles in Florida recently signed a treaty, are the only tribe that have never signed a peace treaty with the United States.

They live in poverty. Now their national sport is croquet (this is true, incidentally).

There was a small settlement of these Indians living in shacks off the road between her house and the town. In the little village a baby was born to an unmarried Indian woman who died in childbirth.

The old lady offered to care for the child, and on a happy autumn afternoon the baby girl was brought to her by the Indians.

The old lady adored the child.

She would get right down on the floor, too, and play with her; and she was particularly lax about toilet training so that the child was four or five years old before she learned to use an ordinary bathroom.

And at first the old lady had many daydreams. She thought how wonderful it was going to be to educate her, to turn her to great books, to the great paintings, and the mass of music, to the wonders of civilization.

For herself it would be to renew many old acquaintances.

However, after a while the old lady realized that her daydreams were never to be realized. For the child was a . . . well, there's nothing wrong with it, it's actually a very common occurrence even among the best families, it was just that the child was a . . . moron.

She didn't love the child any the less because of it; she showered the growing child with attention and affection.

And the old lady just didn't die. She lived another twenty

years until she was ninety. Then finally she did die.

The bulk of her estate she left to museums, for the girl plainly wasn't suited for the responsibilities which wealth entails; she left a small trust fund ensuring the girl's comfort for life, but not so much as to attract trouble to her.

The girl did not weep at the funeral; instead, a frown (and not an unattractive one!) appeared . . . a thoughtful expression began growing over her face; and afterward she took a long walk, a ceremony she would continue throughout her life.

The girl wasn't smart, but she was smart enough to know she wasn't very smart.

She realized that somehow she had been a disappointment to her grandmother. (She always thought of the old lady as her grandmother.) Her grandmother would have liked it better if she had been an artist of some sort, a writer, perhaps. As she recalled her life and her grandmother's love, a pang of pain at her failing throbbed through her. Something. She wanted to do something. Something her grandmother would like, to show her, something that would please her. What gift can be taken to a grave?

She decided she would become a writer.

However at twenty the poor girl had still never read anything other than comic books and "true confessions" magazines.

Well, she decides she's going to be a writer . . . what that meant to her was that she should write true confession stories. Only . . . when she read those things she actually believed them, she actually thought they were *true*, and not just formula stories written by hack writers.

Well, if she's going to write a true confessions story she has to have something to confess, but she has nothing to write about, so she decides what she needs is some "experience"; so she goes to Chicago and finds a bar that to her looks "evil-looking," picks up a guy, and sure enough, he steals her money, and does her wrong.

So the girl went home and wrote a true confession, telling it exactly as it had occurred.

And as she'd never read anything other than "true confessions" magazines, this was the way her mind worked, and she automatically wrote in their style, so that when an editor read her story, he accepted it, simply assuming the author's name was a pseudonym of a professional.

It never occurred to the editor that what he was reading was actually true. Had he known, of course, he never would have published it. They don't publish "those kinds of things."

So she wrote more stories, and for each story she went out and had an "experience." And oh all kinds of things happened to her for she picked her men carefully for their literary value, seeking always someone sinister for her unhappy romances, and after each she would simply write what happened, the simple truth in a sorry style.

She began to earn quite a good living, and soon discovered she had a lot of money, which, luckily, she turned over to her grandmother's lawyers, who, by chance, were honest; and who saw to it her income tax was properly paid, and her own money put in a solid savings account. She never spent any of this, though, explaining to her lawyers once that "I do not write for money."

She decided she was ready to begin a broader project, a novel. So she came to New York City, and began living with a guy, and every day when he was out, she'd work on her novel, simply writing what happened, day by day.

When she finished the novel she left him.

And he was not a little confused at her leaving, for though he'd been living on her money, and in fact, victimizing her, or so he figured, he found he had grown fond of her. Other men were to be similarly startled at her sudden leavings, at discovering themselves alone, and would share this perplexity.

But the novel was a great success.

The critics raved. "What humor! What satire! What ironies! What burlesque!" none of them imagining for a minute that what they read was not written with those intentions at all, but was a simple, serious relating of a world she saw.

The book became a best-seller, a book club bought it, a movie was made of it, a smash hit, and it received Academy Awards.

So she wrote more books. Each had a similar success. And for each she would go out and find some guy, some jerk, and would live with him until her novel was completed.

By chance she had an intelligent publisher who advised her to entirely avoid meeting literary people and literary critics, and so protected her from what would have been fatal interviews; and he explained that she was a shy genius, a delicate and rare recluse; and though she always wrote under her real name, he let it be known to the press that this was a pseudonym; and her own acquaintances, to whom she never claimed to be a writer, and who knew her dullness and simple-minded generosities, couldn't conceive of it; but the publisher himself was a little puzzled at how amenable she was to this plan, although she did once explain to him, "I do not write for fame."

It is said here in America that there is nothing sure except death and taxes.

And to be sure, it was not her literary work that embedded her name in the popular mind, but was rather a prosaic noticing by one of her grandmother's old lawyers that she was a member of that Indian tribe that had never signed a treaty with the government, and so was not required to pay taxes.

She'd had half a dozen best-sellers, and they'd made as many movies from them, and, as she already had an income from her grandmother's trust fund, the millions of dollars she had earned had almost entirely gone for taxes, and the government found itself in the position of having to refund quite literally millions of dollars to her.

One day, she had just finished a novel, and had packed her bags and sent them uptown to a hotel—she had left her man, and she was feeling wonderful. (She always felt exhilarated after finishing a work, she'd once told her publisher.)

It was autumn.

She began to walk, as she liked to do, through the city aimlessly, and discovered herself downtown near the Brooklyn Bridge. She decided to walk across the bridge.

Just as she stepped onto the bridge the sky turned yellow, and the wind began to blow, and she looked above and saw the clouds moving fast across the sky, and in the afternoon distance there was a flash from lightning.

If, at this moment one could view the bridge from above you would have seen that at that moment, all the people walking on the bridge that were on the Manhattan side had suddenly turned back to Manhattan, and those on the

Brooklyn side were now hurrying back toward Brooklyn, all rushing to get off the bridge before the storm broke. Finally, only she continued to walk toward the center of the bridge.

She thought it was wonderful. The lightning. The electric air. The booming foghorns and the thunder. "How great!" she laughed. "A storm!"

So that finally when she got to the very center of the Brooklyn Bridge, she was the only person on it.

She looked out over the city and saw a huge gray curtain moving slowly toward her . . . it was the rain she saw, of course, dissolving the city as it approached her.

The very opposite of running from it, she held up her arms to the coming rain, welcoming it, and said, "Ah! What a *grand* thing it is . . . to be an artist!"

Bullfinch & Goblin

❋　　❋

❋

ONCE upon a time there was a bullfinch.

This bullfinch lived in a marsh and on the edge of the marsh there was a cottage.

In the cottage was a family—a mother, a father and a couple of kids—young children.

The bullfinch loved these children very much. He liked to watch them playing in the yard, running around, chasing each other, and sometimes when they went for walks he'd follow them, but their shouting and screaming frightened him because, you know, bullfinches are shy—so he never came close.

One day they sat under a tree talking quietly.

The bird wondered what they were talking about.

He mustered his courage and flew to a branch of the tree and began to listen.

As a matter of fact they were talking about birds.

One of them said, "I wonder how many different kinds of birds there are?"

The older one answered, "Oh, there are sparrows. They sing cheep cheep cheep."

You know, he tried to imitate a sparrow.

"There are owls. They go whoo . . . whooooooo."

"And crows. Caw . . ."

"Bluebirds. Tweet—tweet—tweet—tweet—"

"And woodpeckers. Knock! Knock! Knock! Knock!"

Silence.

"And ducks!" cried the younger one. "Wuaaank! Wuaaank! . . . But aren't there any other kinds of birds?"

"I can't think of any. I guess that's the only kinds of birds there are."

Yi! the bullfinch flew away in a flurry. Here he'd loved these children so much and they didn't even know he existed!

He began to mope around the marsh, and he began to look at himself, and he realized he wasn't very big, and his feathers weren't very bright, but the main thing was he couldn't sing like the other birds.

Moodily he stared into a muddy pool . . . at his own reflection, when up suddenly from the slime oozed a goblin.

Ordinarily the bullfinch would have flown right away, because goblins are little and dirty and ugly and all covered with mud—mud dripping from their outlandish clothes, and, you know, goblins are a little scary—but he was feeling too depressed.

"What's wrong, my friend?" asked the goblin gently. "You seem sad."

He told the goblin all his troubles . . . he wasn't very big . . . and his feathers . . . but the main thing was he couldn't sing like the other birds . . . and gee . . .

"Well as a matter of fact," said the goblin, "I happen to be a very good voice teacher. I can teach you to sing and your voice will be the most beautiful in the whole marsh. However, I want to warn you I am a very strict teacher. You will have to obey me absolutely. The lessons would take a year."

The bullfinch thought it over and he decided to do it.

They went far off to a lonely place out on the great

marsh and began the lessons.

The goblin was a very strict teacher.

He made the bullfinch go on a diet.

He corrected his posture, and taught him how to breathe properly; and in fading light of evening the bullfinch had liked to fly around, high, doing loop the loops, swooping, gliding, doing figure eights for the fun of it; but the goblin said, "None of that nonsense! You have to spend your time at your lessons."

Nights fell quicker.

The bullfinch sang on in the dark.

In the falling whiteness he fasted and shivered: usually he went south at this season.

But the goblin was comfortable cold.

He was covered with dirty icicles which clung at wrong angles to his clothes and fingers and face. He liked to rattle them.

And spring came. Other years at this time the bird had flown out and found a bullfinch hen, built a nest, had baby bullfinches; but the goblin said, "No. You must devote this time to perfecting your art."

The bullfinch continued his lessons restlessly.

The goblin was a great teacher. The voice from the first grew more beautiful, fuller—grander until finally . . .

He flew all night over the marsh to the place where the cottage was, and he arrived just at dawn, just as the sun rose.

He flew to the window ledge of the children's bedroom, and he began to sing!

How he sang!

No one had ever heard singing like that before in the marsh.

The children woke, and they looked, and they saw the

bullfinch, and they ran into their parents' bedroom shouting.

"Daddy! Daddy!" they shriek—"There's a goblin on the
windowsill!"

The Music Copyist

✳   ✳
✳

ONCE upon a time there was a music copyist.

He made copies of scores, and he was good at his business, competent and reliable, and worked free-lance for the best symphonies and performers.

One day he had a rush job. He'd been working ten hours straight on scores for a man considered by the World to be the master of the viola.

It was evening when he finished, and he bundled the big music sheets in a fold of newspaper, and took a cab from his mid-Manhattan apartment to Long Island to the house of the Master Violist.

He arrived about ten in the evening and he found a festive party in progress.

He handed the music to the Master Violist who glanced over it casually and thanked him, and said, "Well, as long as you're here, why don't you take off your overcoat and have a drink."

The music copyist took off his coat and he got his drink, and he stood holding it.

But he felt a little out of place because here he was surrounded by high music society, diamonded people, millionaires and heiresses, dressed in tuxedos and clothes from Paris, while he had ink smudges on his thumbs and cuffs, and he was bleary-eyed from working ten hours, and he was dressed in a regular suit.

The Master began to speak of his hobby which was collecting programs of great musicians performing great music, and a small crowd of people gathered around him to hear him talk, and the music copyist joined the crowd and listened.

The Master finally led the group upstairs to his den to view his collection, and oh! here on the walls were programs of Casals soloing in Madrid, of Albert Schweitzer playing the organ in Africa, Paganini's first and last public performances (framed side by side), Handel conducting the Palace Band for a wedding in England, Bach playing Buxtehude, oh! and more and more. . . .

Finally the music copyist spoke up. Suddenly, and in a little loud voice, he said, "You know, I have a program which deserves to be in this collection."

"Oh," said the Master.

"Yes, and as a matter of fact, I have it right here." The music copyist pulled out his thick wallet and fished down into it among the many torn scraps of paper on which were scrawled telephone numbers and addresses, and he pulled out a tiny folded-up square of paper which he unfolded carefully, and which turned out to be a mimeographed program of a music teacher's recital of her pupils.

He handed it to the Master Violist, who, after glancing at it, said, "What's this?"

"Let me tell you about it," said the music copyist.

"Several years ago I went home . . . to Octagon, Ohio. . . . I hadn't had any occasion to visit my home town in oh ten years. . . . I stayed there at the house of my cousin. . . . Her young son was studying the recorder and I noticed at the time that he really seemed to enjoy his lessons . . . not like most kids his age . . . he actually seemed to enjoy it. . . . One

night the teacher . . . his music teacher was a woman . . .
she also had a choir . . . was to give a recital of her pupils.
. . . My cousin invited me to come along, but I didn't want
to go. . . . Perhaps I should explain that, although I'm not
a musician, I am, in a way, in that business . . . and I have
an ear . . . for instance, I can name any performer on a
recording by his style . . . that is, I mean, of course . . . the
great musicians . . . and I have a record collection that is
one of the . . . ah . . . of which I'm proud. . . . Anyway I
didn't want to hear any *music teacher's* . . . well anyway
. . . I went, mostly to please my cousin, and resolved to try
not to be sarcastic. . . . My cousin drove to the small-town
auditorium. . . . I escorted her to some seats, and we sat
waiting an interminably long time for the thing to begin,
and while we waited I glanced over the program I'd been
given (that one you're holding there in your hand) . . . and
I noticed the music was entirely old music . . . pieces by
Bach and Handel, Couperin, Vivaldi, Scarlatti, and Fresco-
baldi and . . . well it was all good music, but they were
simple things, not technically very difficult, suitable for children to perform. . . . The recital began . . . and after a while
I realized that I was sort of enjoying it . . . and was glad I'd
come. . . . The children weren't prodigies any of them . . .
but the kids played with such a spirit, with such an obvious
joyousness that the whole thing—little sour notes and all—
was transformed for me into pleasure . . . there even seemed
an appropriateness to those little sour notes like a crow's
caw or a frog's croak among country morning finch songs
. . . in fact I became so absorbed in the music that when,
during an intermission, my cousin, sparkling-eyed proud
mother, exclaimed, "Wasn't he wonderful!" I stared at her
blankly wondering exactly what on earth she was talking

about, until I realized I hadn't distinguished her son, and had just been listening, rather than watching. . . . Finally . . . just before the last number the music teacher stepped between the curtains and made an announcement. . . . She said there had been a change in the program and that instead of "Two Songs" by Vivaldi, that the choir would sing the *St. Matthew Passion*, by Johann Sebastian Bach. . . . Well I remember I frowned, a little irritated by the announcement, because I knew what she had said was simply incorrect . . . because the great *St. Matthew Passion* takes four hours to perform . . . it's one of the few greatest and among the most complex pieces of music ever written, and only the best professional choirs ever attempt it . . . and besides it takes a full orchestra to perform it. . . . But then I became distracted by some usherettes, high school girls, moving down the two aisles handing out things, and whispering loudly to the first person in each row, 'Take one of each and pass them on!' . . . which I did, and I found I had in my hands a pointed paper hat—a dunce cap—and a light wooden stick with short crepe paper streamers attached at the top. . . . Well I noticed everyone else was putting on their dunce caps so I put mine on too and sat there clutching the little stick and I remember the thousands of little streamers made a funny quiet noise in the warm summer auditorium air like autumn leaves stirring. . . . Then every light dimmed out . . . and the dunce caps turned on . . . they were luminous . . . the paper streamers too . . . and I looked above and saw dim purple bulbs which I realized was the black light source causing the luminosity. . . . All the dunce caps were shining sea-blue . . . except . . . directly in front of me there was a line of bright white dunce caps . . . and I glanced to the right and left and noticed everyone in my row were wearing white hats . . . and I stared around in back and all the caps were blue except that directly behind me stretched another line of white dunce caps. . . . The white caps formed the design of a Cross. . . . I looked at my own hat . . . it was white . . . and suddenly realized I was wearing the center cap . . . it was just an accident, I just happened to be sitting in that seat . . . but before I could think much about it the choir began to trickle one by one from between the closed curtains wearing luminous brown robes—hands, face and feet invisible, finally forming a solid brownly shining blot across the front of the stage. . . . Then the music teacher appeared on the center dais . . . a silhouette . . . and after the applause there followed the silence . . . broken by a creaking noise which sounded as if the curtains in back of the boys were opened . . . but the stage itself was in complete darkness . . . nothing was visible beyond the bright brown blot. . . . The choir accompanied by a full orchestra began to sing the great *St. Matthew Passion.* . . . The children were trained! they sang . . . but the orchestra . . . they were playing ancient instruments . . . real Bach trumpets, thirteen feet long! shawms! viola da gambas! dull tabors! the actual instruments for which Bach wrote that Passion . . . but their performance! I had never before in my life heard anything nearly like it . . . they were like a band of angels. . . . But then for a moment I remembered something . . . an incident . . . I hadn't paid any attention to it at the time but . . . that afternoon I'd gone out to buy cigarettes and I happened to glance in a window of a car stopped for a light and thought I recognized a French horn player . . . a great musician I'd always thought, but he'd never become well-known . . . I'd done work for him several times, hadn't charged him much because I liked him and admired him and I knew he couldn't afford . . . but then the light changed and the car drove on, and I said to myself, 'Oh, it couldn't have been. What would he be doing here in Octagon?' . . . But now I listened to the ibbletorks . . . yes . . . I became sure . . . my friend was playing in that orchestra! . . . For the next four hours, throughout the complete performance of the *St. Matthew Passion*, I lived in the wonderful daze, listening. . . . Finally it finished, and a few lights went on. . . .

"But the audience . . . the way they reacted . . . it was very strange . . . very peculiar . . . you see—

"Nobody clapped.

"Nobody whistled, or shouted—Bravo!

"Nobody moved, or got up to go home.

"For the phosphorescent fish who live four miles deep in the depths of the ocean off the coast of Japan know no silence as tranquil as that which they left in the dark air of the concert hall.

"Almost one by one the audience began to stream up the aisles toward the entrance, and I got up also . . . and began to work my way through the crowd in the opposite direction. . . . I was moving toward the stage and toward a door at the side which I knew would lead backstage . . . the music teacher appeared in the doorway . . . she was standing there blocking the way . . . and so I just said I wanted to go in and say hello to my friend . . . the French horn player . . . and I named his name and explained that I was a friend of his from New York. . . . She looked puzzled and said, 'What do you mean?' . . . and so I explained again, the French horn player, he was a friend of mine, I just wanted to stop in and say hello, if you'd give him my name I'm sure he'll want to see me, we're good friends. . . . Her face was puzzled and she frowned, and repeated, '*What do you*

mean?' . . . I didn't know what else to say . . . I was looking
puzzled at her . . . she was looking at me, I felt, the way
one looks at an insane person, and finally she said, 'I'm sorry
. . . only performers are allowed back here' . . . and she
stepped inside and the door closed. . . . I walked out of the
theater and got into the car where my cousin sat waiting.
. . . It had been ten o'clock, the regular concert almost finished, when the *Passion* had begun and now it was two in
the morning . . . the kid was already asleep in the back of
the car . . . my cousin drove . . . finally I said, 'Well didn't
you notice anything—strange—about the concert?' . . . and
she answered, 'Yes, it's nonsense her keeping the children
up this late at night! Just nonsense!' . . . 'But the *music*—
who was playing?' . . . 'Oh!' she said, 'I think it's a little
band from Lopert down the highway that comes over to
help her out occasionally at her recitals.' . . . But I knew
that I hadn't been listening to any little band from *Lopert,*
Ohio . . . and then I said, 'But what about all those lights
. . . that Cross . . . what did it all mean?' . . . And my cousin
laughed, 'Oh, she's always doing crazy things like that . . .
you can see why the children love her.' . . .

"Well, that's all."

The music copyist looked around the den at the silent
group.

"The story's finished.

"I left Octagon that morning and haven't returned. That
program, that program there, that's the program from that
night . . . look . . . see! . . . the last number on the program.
It says, 'Two Songs,' by Vivaldi. . . ."

"Ooooh!" said a voice sarcastically.

"Stop it!" said someone with a disgusted wave.

"Come down, mister!" snarled a beautiful girl.

The group turned downstairs, mumbled asides answered by grimaces, and the Master himself made a very nasty, biting comment which the music copyist couldn't help but overhear.

The music copyist turned white. Nobody believed his story.

He asked for his coat from a butler, and had to wait a long time for it, and then pushed his way through the laughing, drinking bunches toward the door, and just as he stepped outside—the Master Violist appeared in the doorway behind him.

"Let me walk you a ways," he said.

The Master took the copyist's arm as they walked and he said, "I'd like to apologize for what I had to say on the stairway back there. Look . . . by chance you heard something you weren't intended to hear. I know you heard what you heard, but please . . . just *don't talk* about it. Those people," he said with a gesture back at his brightly lit, noisy house, "they can't understand."

The Master's fingers tightened around the copyist's arm, tightened with a violist's grasp, with all the strength in a violist's fingers, and he whispered, "But that night! that night in Octagon—wasn't it great! Wasn't it great!"

The copyist jerked his arm away. He was rubbing it gingerly, and said, "Yes, certainly, but how do *you* know?"

"I was there, of course," answered the Master, and then he said (and did he really blush proudly in the moonlight as he said it?): "I was playing second viola."

The Hidden Ballroom at Versailles

✳   ✳
✳

ELEGANT and opulent, yet undiscovered, "the hidden ball-
room" at Versailles whose entire floor is made with many
fragile panes into a smooth, single surface of mirror, rests
undusty in darkness, unentered for two centuries by a
flicker, nary a moonbeam nor match, lamp, nor any light,
except for one time. Then, a tiny batch of insect eggs
(blown through a crevice down through an imperfection
in the molding onto the great glass floor) hatched fireflies.

That was in 1893.